HILDA™ © 2019 Hilda Productions Limited, a Silvergate Media company.

Hilda and the Hidden People © Flying Eye Books 2019.

This paperback edition published in 2019.
First published in 2018 by Flying Eye Books, an imprint of Nobrow Ltd.
27 Westgate Street, London E8 3RL.

Written by Stephen Davies and illustrated by Seaerra Miller,
based on the characters and storylines
created by Luke Pearson and Silvergate Media company.

1 3 5 7 9 10 8 6 4 2

Published in the US by Nobrow (US) Inc.

Printed and bound in Great Britain by Clays Ltd,
Elcograf S.p.A. on FSC® certified paper.

ISBN: 978-1-912497-88-1

www.flyingeyebooks.com

Based on the Hildafolk series of graphic novels by Luke Pearson

HiLDA
AND THE HiDDEN
PEOPLE

Written by Stephen Davies   Illustrated by Seaerra Miller

FLYING EYE BOOKS

London | New York

THE CAVES
OF KISMET

THE GREAT
WATERFALL

TROLL ROCK

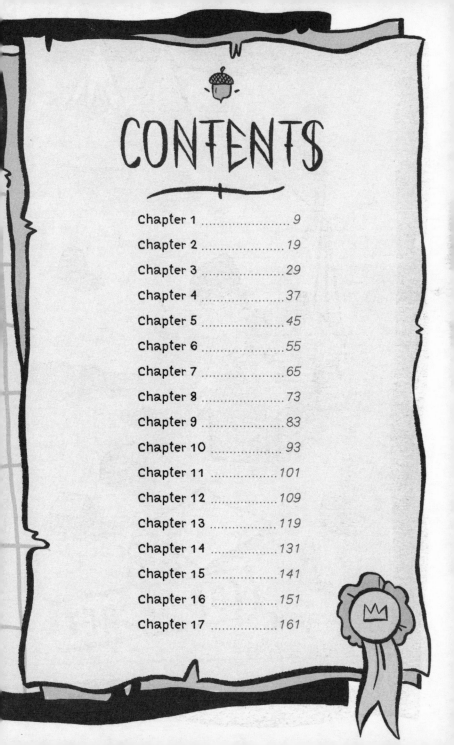

CONTENTS

1

The wind blew. The woffs flew. The sun sank low in the sky. High on the south side of Boot Mountain a little girl with blue hair sat on a rock, sticking her tongue out.

Hilda always stuck her tongue out when she was drawing. It helped her concentrate. The tip of her pencil darted across her sketchbook as she drew the forests and plains, the waterfalls and rivers, the snowcapped mountains and the lush green valley. Making maps was an important part of an adventurer's job, and adventuring was something Hilda took very seriously indeed.

As soon as she finished drawing the mountains, Hilda gave them names based on what they looked like. In her neatest handwriting she labeled Mug Mountain, Lamp Mountain, Moon Mountain, Beetle Mountain, Bottle Mountain, and Bobblehat Mountain. It was turning out to be an excellent map, even if she said so herself. And she had to say so herself, because there was no one else for miles around, unless you counted Twig, and he couldn't talk.

Twig was a deer fox, a small white bundle of courage and cuteness who often accompanied Hilda on her adventures.

Down below them in the middle of the plain was an enormous standing rock. Hilda stared at it, shielding her eyes from the slanting rays of the afternoon sun. The strangest thing about the rock was the long, pointy stone that stuck straight out of it. Like a handle on a saucepan, thought Hilda. Or a long nose on an ugly face.

Hilda's blood ran cold. She shrugged her adventuring satchel off her shoulders and pulled out the book *CAVES AND THEIR UNFRIENDLY OCCUPANTS* by Emil Gammelplassen, flicking through the pages until she reached the section on trolls.

Some species of troll cannot stand sunlight. If the sun's rays fall on such a troll, it turns to stone. It can be difficult to tell a normal standing rock from a troll rock, but you might notice hints of a face, in particular a long nose-like protrusion. At sunset it turns back into a troll again.

Hilda stared at the troll rock. She had never seen one before and she could hardly believe that it was right there in front of her.

CAVES AND THEIR UNFRIENDLY OCCUPANTS

A prudent traveler will take care when approaching a standing rock or boulder, as it is just as likely to be a troll rock awaiting nightfall. If this is the case, there is no cause for alarm, as the troll will stay in this form so long as it is in contact with daylight. Because of their aversion to sunlight, trolls make their homes in dark places such as caves or tunnels. While it would be unnecessary for an adventurer to avoid such places altogether for fear of trolls, it is worthwhile to proceed with exceptional caution and careful preparation.

any trolls are quite indifferent to the presence of humans, or at the very least are as wary of humans as humans are of them. There are some species, however, which do prefer humans as their main source of food, and are surprisingly clever in their preparation of human-based cuisine. Knowing this to be the case, it is wise when traversing troll territory to carry a bell, the sound of which is widely known to be agonizing to trolls of all species.

"What do you think, Twig?" asked Hilda. "Quick sketch of the troll rock while we have the chance?"

Twig wagged his tail cheerfully. He was always up for an adventure.

Hilda pulled her yellow scarf tight around her neck, hoisted her adventuring satchel onto her back, and broke into a run.

A few minutes later Hilda and Twig were standing in front of the troll rock. Now that she was close enough to examine it properly, she could make out not just the nose but also two oval-shaped cracks in the rock that looked for all the world like glaring eyes.

She took from her adventuring satchel a little bell on a loop of string. "Here's a job for you, Twig," she said. "Hang this on its nose. If the troll starts to move, the jingling of the bell will warn us."

Twig took the bell in his mouth. He scampered up the body of the troll rock, tiptoed along

the horizontal nose and looped the bell over its
pointed end.

Hilda sat down cross-legged on the ground
and began to sketch the craggy outline of the troll
rock. She stuck out her tongue as she drew the
curve of the body, the bulge of the head, and the
long, jutting nose. Then she moved to a different
spot and sketched the whole thing from the side,
then again from the back.

"Not bad," she whispered, examining the
finished sketches. "What do you think, Twig?"

The deer fox cocked his head on one side.

"I know," said Hilda. "The shape of the eyes
isn't quite right, is it? I need to sketch them
close up."

Hilda glanced over at the sun, which was low
in the sky, near to the horizon. She stuffed her
sketchbook down her sweater and removed her
red rubber boots. "Twenty minutes till sunset,"
she murmured. "Plenty of time for one last sketch."

She dug her fingertips into a crevice and hauled

herself up the troll rock's body onto its nose. She was concentrating so hard that she did not see a dark cloud gathering in the west and moving towards the sun.

On the ground below, Twig snarled.

Hilda took the sketchbook from her sweater. "One minute, boy!" she called. "I'll be down just as soon as I've sketched these eyes."

There she sat with her tongue sticking out and her legs hanging down on either side of the troll's nose. Coming up here had been an excellent idea. She could see the precise shape and texture of the troll's wide stony eyes. The glaring eyeballs. The round pupils that seemed to get bigger and brighter with every moment that passed.

Hilda's pencil darted across the paper. On the ground below, Twig yapped and growled.

"I'm sorry, boy!" called Hilda. "I know you're hungry. Just one minute more and we can go home for dinner."

Ding.

"Oh," said Hilda.

Ding-ding.

"Oh dear," said Hilda.

Ding-a-ling-a-ling-a-ling-a-ling.

"Run!" yelled Hilda.

2

Hilda wriggled off the troll's nose and slid down its body onto the ground.

The monster reared up tall. It raked the air with razor-sharp claws and the jingling of the bell on the end of its nose was drowned out by its bloodcurdling roars.

Hilda was already off and running. Twig sprinted at her heels. Together they ran across the plain, dodging boulders and bounding over ditches. The troll lumbered after them. For such a big-bellied creature it was remarkably fast.

"This way, Twig!" yelled Hilda. "If we cross the river we might lose it."

They headed for the crossing point and dashed down the bank. Hilda took the stepping stones two at a time, sailing through the air with great long strides. Twig scampered after her.

The troll ploughed down the bank, slipped on the wet surface of the first stepping stone and fell into the river with a mighty splash.

"Phew," said Hilda. "Safe at last."

But she celebrated too soon. The troll stood up, blew two jets of snotty water from its nostrils, and began to wade towards them through the swirling river.

"The water only comes up to its waist!" cried Hilda. "Run, Twig!"

In the open meadow on the west bank of the

river, a flock of woffs were perched on a circle of stones. As Hilda and Twig dashed past, the woffs rose into the air with a chorus of angry snuffles.

Surrounded on all sides by furry yellow bodies, Hilda could no longer see where she was going. "Hey!" she panted. "Would you mind flying a little bit high— *Aaaaaaaaargh!*"

The ground disappeared beneath her feet and she half fell, half rolled down a steep earthy slope, landing in a heap at the bottom.

"Ouch," she murmured.

She brushed the dirt off her face and opened her eyes. Twig was standing over her, nudging her with his antlers.

"Hey!" Hilda whispered. "Your antlers are sharp, you know."

She looked around. She was lying at the bottom of a gigantic dent in the ground—a crater carpeted with crushed grass and shaped like a clover leaf.

A very *long* clover leaf with four toes.

"It's a footprint!" Hilda whispered. "Look, Twig, it's as wide as a house! Not even forest giants have feet this big."

Twig sniffed at the crushed grass. He growled softly and then the fur on the back of his neck stood up.

"Let's wait here until we're sure the troll has gone," Hilda said. "I can sketch this footprint while we're waiting."

She rummaged in her adventuring satchel, but the sketchbook was not there. She must have dropped it in the panic when the troll rock came to life.

Hilda punched the earth in frustration. She didn't know which she was sorrier to lose, her map or her troll sketches. The troll sketches,

probably. Trolls hardly ever came down onto
the plain. It could be years before she saw
another one.

The sun set and the moon rose round and
bright. They walked around the edge of the
footprint until they came to a patch of tangled
tree roots. Twig jumped onto Hilda's satchel and
she used the roots to haul herself up the side of
the crater, back onto solid ground. She strained
her ears to listen for the jingle of a bell, but all
she heard was the snuffling of woffs and the
gentle babble of the river.

"The troll has gone," she said. "Come on, Twig,
let's go home."

They skirted the blue pine forest, then headed
west across the wilderness. Hilda could see her
house in the distance—a little red cabin at the foot
of Bobblehat Mountain. Home sweet home.

They passed the catfish pond where Hilda
swam in summertime, and the hollow bludbok

tree, which was great for building dens. Orange light shining from the windows of her house told her that Mom had already lit a fire in the hearth. Dinner would be on the table soon. A piping hot stew, most likely, and a big bowl of rowanberries.

Ding-a-ling-a-ling.

Hilda's blood froze. She turned.

Out from the shadow of the bludbok tree stepped the troll. Its eyes shone in the moonlight. Its mouth twisted into a horrible grimace. Its claws reached out towards her.

"Nice knowing you, Twig," whispered Hilda.

The troll waved its stubby arms and roared long and loud, but there was something odd about the sound. It was more of a moan than a roar.

"Listen to that," whispered Hilda. "I think it's in distress."

Suddenly it all made sense. The eyes shining with tears. The mouth twisted in pain. Stubby arms trying to reach the bell on the end of that long nose.

25

Hilda stepped forward. "What's up?" she said. "Is the sound of the bell upsetting you? Are you having trouble taking it off? Don't worry, Mr. Troll, I can fix that for you."

Ignoring Twig's yelps of warning, Hilda darted forward and climbed up the troll. It was smooth like clay and it smelled distinctly of stale bread. Moments later Hilda was perched on the end of the troll's nose, unhooking the bell.

"There," she said, throwing the bell to the ground. "That won't bother you any more."

But as Hilda clambered down the troll's arm and past its hamlike hand, the monster made its move. Huge fingers curled tight around her body and raised her to a gaping mouth.

"No!" wailed Hilda. "You can't do that! I was helping you! I felt sorry for you! Stop it! No!"

The troll's sharp teeth glinted in the moonlight. Its tongue lolled out, blowing foul breath all over Hilda.

"AAAAARGH!" she screamed, closing her eyes.

Nothing happened.

She opened her eyes again. On the tip of the troll's tongue was something she recognized.

"My sketchbook!" cried Hilda, grabbing it with both hands. "You wonderful wonderful creature. Thank you so much! I'd give you a kiss if your breath wasn't so gross."

The troll let out a belchy sigh and lowered her to the ground.

"Thanks again!" Hilda called, as the monster lumbered off across the moonlit wilderness.

3

"Hi, Mom, I'm home!" called Hilda, barging in through the front door and pulling off her red rubber boots. The house was toasty warm, as always, and a divine aroma of ginger, nutmeg, and caraway seeds wafted over her.

"Hilda!" Mom jumped up from her desk. "You were such a long time. How was your day?"

"Overall pretty traumatic," sighed Hilda, hugging her. "But such is the life of an adventurer."

"Casserole's ready," said Mom. She went into the kitchen and came back with two steaming bowls of stew. "Did you draw anything nice for me today?"

Hilda bent low over the bowl and slurped her stew. "I drew a map of the valley."

"May I see?" Mom reached for Hilda's sketchbook. "Ew, it's all wet and sticky, Hilda. What have you been doing with it?"

Hilda bent even lower over her bowl, pretending not to have heard the question.

Mom opened the book to Hilda's map of the valley. "Bobblehat Mountain," she chuckled. "Yes, I suppose it does look a bit like a bobblehat, with a really tiny bobble. Good job, Hilda."

From over by the fire came a doleful voice. "The mountains already have names, you know, if you can be bothered to do the research."

Hilda jumped, and craned her neck to see who had spoken. Lying down next to the fire was a little wooden man with a coconut-shaped head and big mournful eyes.

"Hey!" cried Hilda. "Who let him in here?"

"He's harmless," said Mom. "To be honest, I didn't even know he was there."

"That's my point." Hilda flung her arms up in disgust. "He always wanders in uninvited. It's rude!"

"Perhaps he's lonely."

"Of course he's lonely. He's a total weirdo."

"It's true, he is a bit strange." Mom picked up her bowl and slurped the last few mouthfuls of her stew. "But remember, we must seem strange to the various magical creatures who live in this valley. Do you want some rowanberries?"

"Yes, please."

"Besides," Mom added, "the Wood Man always brings us logs for the fire. That's not rude. That's kind. And as I always say, kindness is the most importa— HILDA, WHAT IS THIS?!"

Mom had turned over another page of Hilda's sketchbook and was staring goggle-eyed at Hilda's drawings of the troll rock.

"It's a troll rock," said Hilda. "I've never seen one before. I couldn't resist doing a few quick drawings."

"A FEW?! YOU MEAN THERE'S MORE?" Mom turned over another page, then another, then another. Her nostrils quivered with anger. "HILDA! HOW DID YOU GET SUCH A CLOSE-UP DRAWING OF ITS EYES?"

"I'm not sure. I *might* have stood on its nose to draw that one."

"YOU STOOD ON A TROLL'S NOSE! WHAT IF THE SUN HAD SET WHILE YOU WERE DRAWING? WHAT IF A BIG CLOUD HAD PASSED OVERHEAD?"

Hilda opened her mouth to reply, then shut it again. Sometimes silence was the best course of action.

"I'LL TELL YOU EXACTLY WHAT WOULD HAVE HAPPENED, YOUNG LADY. IF THAT TROLL HAD WOKEN UP IT WOULD HAVE DEVOURED YOU IN ONE BIG GULP—LIKE THIS." Mom tipped back her head and dropped a rowanberry down her throat. "OMNOMNOM, VERY NICE. TASTIEST LITTLE GIRL I'VE EATEN ALL YEAR. OMNOMNOMNOMNOMNOMNOM—"

Knock, knock.

"I'll get it!" called Hilda.

She ran to the door and opened it. A tiny envelope lay on the doorstep.

"Oh no," said Hilda. "That's the sixth one this week." She fetched a magnifying glass from Mom's desk drawer and unfolded the letter.

"*To the Occupiers*," she read out loud. "*On behalf of the hidden people of the Northern Elven Counties, we demand that you vacate these premises forthwith. Failure to comply with this demand will set in motion a forcible eviction process culminating in the comminution of aforesaid premises.*" Hilda frowned. "What is 'comminution', Mom?"

"It means smashing something up into tiny pieces," said Mom. "What they're saying is, if we don't move out they'll chuck us out and smash our house up."

"Ha!" said Hilda. "I'd like to see them try."

"That's the spirit," said Mom, but her face wore a worried frown.

That evening they sat on the sofa in front of the roaring fire. They toasted marshmallows and played Hilda's favorite board game, Dragon

Panic. Twig dozed on the rug at Hilda's feet.

SMASH*!*

A pebble flew through the window, bounced off Twig's head and landed on the rug. Twig raised his head and blinked in surprise.

Hilda ran to the door and yanked it open.

"HEY, YOU, WHATEVER YOU ARE!" she yelled at the top of her voice. "DO YOU THINK IT'S FUNNY TO THROW STONES THROUGH PEOPLE'S WINDOWS? WELL, IT'S NOT! IT'S VERY BAD MANNERS. GO AWAY AND THINK ABOUT WHAT YOU'VE DONE AND THEN GO TO TROLBERG ON THE TRAIN AND BUY US A NEW WINDOW!"

The wind howled. The rain lashed down. Hilda closed the door and went back to the sofa.

SMASH*!* CRASH*!* CLATTER*!*

Dozens of pebbles smashed through the windows and rained down on them like hail.

"Take cover!" shouted Mom.

4

Hilda dived beneath an armchair. Mom took cover under the sofa. Twig jumped onto the coffee table and stood there in the middle of the Dragon Panic board, growling and snarling.

"Attention, residents!" announced a stern voice. "Having provided adequate warning and opportunity to cooperate, on behalf of the hidden people of the Northern Elven Counties, we shall now implement your forcible eviction from the premises."

"Oh no," whispered Hilda. "This is the part where they chuck us out and smash our house up, right?"

As Hilda stared at the shattered windows, a vase of flowers on one of the window sills caught her eye. Through the curve of the vase she glimpsed the shadow of a tiny person wearing a tiny hat.

"Look there," she whispered. "That shadow!"

But before Mom could see anything, the vase

teetered and toppled and started to fall.

"My favorite vase!" cried Mom.

The half-full bag of marshmallows rose off the coffee table and flew into the fire.

"Hey!" cried Hilda. "We were eating those!"

The invisible invaders ignored all protests and proceeded to smash up picture frames, ornaments, plates, and bowls. They ripped up books, knocked board games off shelves, and pushed the TV off its stand.

Then they turned their attention to Hilda
and Mom.

"Argh!" cried Hilda. "They're all over me!
I can feel them, like ants!"

"Make a run for it!" shouted Mom.

Mom was right. The sensible course of action
was to get out of the house, run for the mountains,
and not to look back.

As Hilda crawled out from underneath the
armchair and sprinted towards the door, the
invisible people gave a tiny cheer of victory.

Hilda stopped and whirled around. "OH,
REALLY?" she yelled. "YOU THINK YOU'VE WON,
DO YOU? I'LL SHOW YOU!"

She sprinted to the broom cupboard and
pulled out an enormous broom. "LISTEN UP, YOU
PESKY PINHEADS!" she shrieked. "ON BEHALF
OF THE HUMANS OF MY HOUSE I SHALL NOW
IMPLEMENT YOUR FORCIBLE EVICTION FROM
THE PREMISES!"

In a blind rage, Hilda dashed all around the

living room and kitchen, pushing the broom in front of her. The air filled with clouds of dust and tiny cries of panic. *Eek! Arg! Oof! Eee!*

"Get out!" cried Hilda, sweeping faster and harder. "Get out! Get out! Get out! Get out! Get out! Get out! Get out! Get out! Get out! Get out! Get out!" She swept the invisible people across the floor and out onto the doorstep. "AND STAY OUT!" she yelled, slamming the door.

Hilda turned back into the room, breathing hard. Mom was standing by the dinner table, staring at her, openmouthed.

"That was awesome," said Mom. "Kind of scary too."

Hilda felt weak in the knees. "I need to sit down," she said in a small voice.

Mom brought her a chair. "I'll make us some hot chocolate," she said.

"I'll have one too, if you're making some," called a doleful voice.

Hilda turned towards the sound. Over in the far

corner of the room, with his nose in a book about giants, lay the Wood Man.

"You!" cried Hilda. "Are you still here?"

"I was trying to read," said the Wood Man, "but you were making an awful lot of noise."

"You could have helped us," said Hilda. "After all, you're basically part of the family now."

"No, I'm not," said the Wood Man, putting his nose back in his book.

While Hilda and the Wood Man drank their hot chocolate, Mom swept up the broken glass.

"We can't stay here," Mom said. "Not if this is going to keep happening. We'll have to move house."

Hilda frowned. "But there aren't any other houses in the valley."

"I was thinking of Trolberg."

"No!" cried Hilda. "We've always lived in the wilderness. I love it here."

"We can't stay if we're being attacked, Hilda."

"Yes, but—"

"But nothing," said Mom. "Finish your hot chocolate and go to bed, Hilda. We can talk about it in the morning."

Hilda put down her mug, grabbed a broken pencil, and tore a page from her sketchbook.

> DEAR INVISIBLE LITTLE GUYS WHO TRASHED
> MY HOUSE, WHY ARE YOU SO MAD AT ME
> AND MY MOM?
> PLEASE TELL ME, SO I CAN FIX IT AND
> WE CAN ALL LIVE IN PEACE.
>
> FROM HILDA

She slipped the note into an envelope, put it out on the doorstep, and went upstairs to bed.

Adventurers don't cry, Hilda told herself as she snuggled down beneath the blankets. But it was hard work being an adventurer all the time. Sometimes you just needed to take a few minutes' break.

"PSSST! Hilda!"

Hilda woke with a start and switched on her bedside lamp. "Who's there?" she said.

"I'm one of the little people who trashed your house."

Hilda's heart skipped a beat. She jumped to her feet and raised her pillow above her head. "Get out!" she shouted.

"The trashing wasn't done by me personally," said the little voice. "I'm more of a writer than a fighter."

"Did you read my note?"

"Yes. I want us to be friends."

Hilda wondered if she was dreaming. The little voice seemed to be coming from right inside her head. She poked a finger in one ear and waggled it about.

"Careful with that finger!" cried the little voice. "I'm sitting in your ear. Now, if you'll just go over to your desk, you'll find all the relevant forms."

"What forms?"

"The forms that will allow you to see me."

Hilda looked at the mess on her desk: sketchbooks, pencils, markers, tape, monster-shaped erasers, and, right there on the edge, a teetering stack of tiny papers.

"I've filled out most of it already," said the little voice. "You just need to sign the top page."

Hilda sharpened a pencil and signed on the dotted line.

"Good," said the voice. "Now your house is officially mine."

"WHAT?"

"Just kidding," said the voice. "But you should never ever sign something without reading it first, you know. Luckily for you, I am an extremely honest elf. You can see me now, by the way."

Hilda went over to the mirror and looked closely at her right ear. Perched on her earlobe was a tiny elf with a pointy red hat and pointy shoes.

"Name's Alfur," said the elf, grinning.

"I see," said Hilda, smiling sweetly. "So now that we're friends, Alfur, there is one teeny little thing you could do for me."

"What's that?"

"GO AND TELL YOUR PEOPLE TO STOP SENDING US HORRIBLE LETTERS AND THROWING STONES THROUGH OUR WINDOWS AND SMASHING OUR VASES AND RIPPING UP OUR BOOKS AND INCINERATING OUR MARSHMALLOWS AND COMMONATING . . . CAMMUNITING . . . CINEMATING . . . WHATEVER . . .

EVERYTHING WE OWN AND MESSING UP OUR
GAME OF DRAGON PANIC, WHICH BY THE WAY
I WOULD HAVE WON IF YOU HADN'T KNOCKED
THE PIECES OFF THE BOARD!"

"Sorry," said Alfur. "But it's complicated,
you see."

"No, it's not."

"Yes, it is," Alfur insisted. "Look out of
the window."

Hilda went to the window, drew back the
curtains, and peered out across the moonlit
wilderness. What she saw there made her stomach
flip over inside her. The wilderness was full of
miniature houses as far as the eye could see.

"No way!" cried Hilda.

She ran downstairs, taking the steps three at
a time, and barged out of the front door without
even stopping to put her boots on.

The elf houses were arranged in clusters, some
on the grass and some on rocks. There was a town
by the bludbok tree and another along the edge of

the catfish pond. The biggest town of all was in front of Hilda's house.

Twig followed her outside, wagging his tail. The deer fox could not see the elf houses and must have wondered what all the fuss was about.

"This is amazing." Hilda knelt down to take a closer look at the little roofs and chimneys and the tiny doors and windows. "They're just like dolls' houses."

"They're nothing at all like dolls' houses," huffed Alfur.

Hilda stared as Twig's back leg somehow passed right through the roof of an elf house without breaking it. "Amazing," she said again.

Most of the windows were dark, but one still had a light on inside.

Hilda picked the house up and peered in through the window. An elf in a comfortable armchair was taking a sip of tea when he saw Hilda's giant eye at the window. He spat his tea across the room and fell out of his chair.

"Do you mind?" said Alfur. "Behavior like that will not endear you to elfkind."

"And what about elfkind's behavior?" shouted Hilda, slamming the little house back down on the grass. "Marshmallows? Vases? TV? Or have you forgotten already?"

"It's our new Prime Minister," Alfur said. "He promised to get rid of you if he was elected, and now he has been elected, so . . . well . . . you know . . . "

"But that's not fair!" shouted Hilda. "My great-grandpa built this cabin a hundred years ago. We're allowed to live here as much as you are!"

"Don't shout at me!" Alfur shouted back. "I agree with you!"

"Take me to the Prime Minister," Hilda said. "I need to fix this quick, before Mom moves us to Trolberg."

Alfur laughed in disbelief. "I can't arrange a meeting with the elf Prime Minister. I wouldn't even know how. I'm a nobody."

Hilda thought hard. "What about the leader of

this town right here?" she asked, pointing at the houses in front of her.

"The Mayor?" Alfur thought for a while. "I suppose I *could* take you to see the Mayor."

"Good," said Hilda. "Let's go right now."

"Yes, let's," said Alfur. "After all, elf mayors love being woken up by blue-haired giant girls in the middle of the night. I'm being sarcastic, if you hadn't noticed."

"Right," said Hilda. "Tomorrow, then."

"Tomorrow, then," said Alfur. He climbed down out of her ear and disappeared into the grass.

Hilda sat down on the doorstep with her head in her hands. She had always loved living in the wilderness with no other houses for miles around. It was a shock to find out that there were not just other houses in the valley but several towns within a stone's throw of her house.

The grandfather clock in the hall chimed midnight. Hilda shivered. The night was chilly and her socks were wet through. She was just about to get up and go inside when a shadow passed through the moonlight.

Hilda looked up and gasped.

A colossal shape loomed above her. It was bigger than her house, bigger than the bludbok tree, bigger even than Bobblehat Mountain. It was so gigantic that Hilda felt dizzy just looking at it.

The black shape gazed down at her from above and its eyes were like twin stars glowing sorrowfully in the night sky.

"Mom," Hilda croaked. "Come and look at this."

She was trying to shout but her voice would not come out properly, and by the time her voice did start working again the giant was gone.

Oh dear, thought Hilda, as she went inside. Mom isn't going to like any of this.

6

The next morning, Hilda talked nonstop as she spread peanut butter on her bread.

"Mom, I saw something strange yesterday. In fact, I didn't just see it—I fell into it. A massive footprint in the soft ground by the river. At first I thought it was a forest giant footprint, but then I realized it was ten times bigger than a forest giant foot. Maybe twenty times bigger!"

"That's more than enough peanut butter, Hilda," said Mom.

"I thought, no, that's impossible, there aren't any giants that big, but guess what? I *saw* it last night, just after I said goodbye to Alfur."

"Too much peanut butter," said Mom. "Put some of it back."

"Did I tell you about Alfur? I don't think I did. He's a little person. He's helping me fix our elf problem."

Mom nodded. "I'm not surprised you had strange dreams last night, after everything that's been happening around here."

"This wasn't a dream, Mom. It happened!"

"Less talking please, and more eating."

Hilda sighed and took a bite of her bread.

After breakfast Hilda brushed her teeth and packed her adventuring satchel.

"Your mom isn't very bright, is she?" said a voice in her ear.

"Yes, she is!" snapped Hilda. "My mom's a graphic designer. She has hundreds of great design

ideas for things. Packaging . . . magazines . . .
lots of stuff. She couldn't do her job if she wasn't
EXTREMELY bright. And anyway, maybe Mom's
right. Maybe I *was* dreaming last night."

"I think not," said Alfur. "Take a look outside."

Hilda went to the front door and opened it. The
elf town was still there—a beautiful mosaic of red
and yellow roofs.

"The Mayor is waiting for you," said Alfur.
"Turn a little to your left and take twelve strides
forward."

Hilda and Twig stalked among the houses,
being careful not to step on any of them.

"Good," said Alfur. "Now bend down and you'll
see a flat rock with an enormous building on it.
That's the Town Hall."

Hilda knelt down. "I don't see any enormous
buildings. I do see a tiny building that's slightly
bigger than all the other tiny buildings."

"Shush," hissed Alfur. "The Mayor will hear
you."

Hilda squinted down at the steps of the Town Hall. On the top step stood a cross-looking elf with pudgy cheeks, wearing a black top hat.

Alfur jumped out of Hilda's ear and slid down a marble column onto the top step of the Town Hall. "Honorable Mayor," he said, bowing. "May I have the pleasure of introducing you to—"

"I know who she is," interrupted the Mayor. "She's the giant! The menace! And we've had enough of her cruel occupation of our historic town. Haven't we, Angelina? Yes, we have. Oh yes, we have."

Hilda wondered who Angelina was. Then she noticed that the Mayor was carrying in his arms a fat brown cat. The cat was trying to jump out of the Mayor's grasp, but the more she wriggled the tighter he cuddled her.

"I'm not a menace," said Hilda. "I didn't even know you existed until recently."

"Pure ignorance," said the Mayor.

"You're INVISIBLE," yelled Hilda.

"Don't shout," said the Mayor. "Angelina here is pregnant and I don't want her to be alarmed. Do I, Angelina? No, I don't. You're much too precious. Alfur, fetch Angelina's basket, will you? She doesn't look very well."

"Certainly, Mr. Mayor." Alfur rushed off to find the basket.

Hilda tried again to reason with the Mayor. "Why do you have to evict us?" she said. "Why can't we live in peace, side by side?"

The Mayor glared up at her. "There's no point talking about it," he said. "The plans for your eviction have already been drawn up. Letters have been sent. Forms have been filled out."

"Then make new forms!" cried Hilda, leaning so far forward that her hair draped across the steps of the Town Hall. "Make new forms that say we don't have to move."

"IT'S NOT THAT SIMPLE!" The Mayor put his cat on the ground and shook his fist at Hilda. "I CAN'T MAKE NEW FORMS JUST BECAUSE

I FEEL LIKE IT!"

"But you're the Mayor!"

"EXACTLY!" The Mayor's cheeks wobbled as he fought to control his anger. "I'm only the Mayor, and the Prime Minister is the Prime Minister, and your eviction is his big idea, not mine. It's out of my hands"—he glanced at his stumpy stick-like arms—"and I don't even have hands."

Hilda scowled. "Then I shall talk to the Prime Minister," she said. "Where can I find him?"

"I'm not telling you," said the Mayor. "That's classified information."

Hilda drew herself up to her full height. "Is that so?"

"Yes."

Alfur came out of the Town Hall clutching a tiny cat basket. "Where's Angelina?" he asked.

The Mayor looked right. The Mayor looked left. The Mayor whirled around, whistling and cooing and making silly kissing noises in his cheeks. Then he glared accusingly at Hilda.

"Where's my kitty?" he demanded.

"I'm not telling you," Hilda replied sweetly. "That's classified information."

"TELL ME!" shrieked the Mayor.

"All right," said Hilda. "She's in my hair. She crawled in there at the same time that you were refusing to tell me where I can find the Prime Minister."

"GIVE HER BACK!"

"I don't know," said Hilda. "She seems like a nice, quiet cat. Perhaps I'll let her live in my hair forever."

"PLEASE!" The Mayor fell to his knees and his top hat fell off, revealing a tiny bald head. "I'M BEGGING YOU!"

Hilda folded her arms. "Where can I find the Prime Minister?"

The Mayor shook his head. "I WILL NEVER TELL YOU!" he sobbed. "DO YOU HEAR ME, GIANT GIRL? I WILL NEVER EVER EVER EVER EVER EVER . . . all right, I'll tell you. The Prime

Minister's headquarters are in the Caves of Kismet behind the Great Waterfall."

"Thank you," said Hilda. "That wasn't so hard, was it?" She reached into her hair, gently removed the cat, which for some reason looked much thinner now, and placed her in her basket. "Goodbye, Mr. Mayor."

She turned and started to walk off.

"Wait for me!" Alfur sprinted down the steps of the Town Hall and leaped onto Hilda's sweater. "May I just say," he huffed, "that was the meanest thing I've ever witnessed. You're a big bully, that's what you are."

Hilda was stung by Alfur's words. No one had ever called her mean before. Or big. Or a bully.

"No, I'm not," she said. "I only did it because—"

"Because what?"

"Because I'm afraid, OK? I was born here. This valley is all I've ever known. I'd rather die than move to Trolberg!"

Alfur climbed onto Hilda's shoulder, swung on her earlobe and hauled himself up into her ear. "Glad to hear it," he muttered, "because from what I've heard about the Caves of Kismet, that is exactly what is going to happen to you."

7

After a calming cup of tea, Hilda set off with Alfur on her quest to reach the Caves of Kismet. They passed the bludbok tree and the catfish pond, then set out across the wilderness towards the river.

"What have you heard about the Caves of Kismet?" asked Hilda.

"Put it this way," said Alfur. "They are extremely difficult to reach. I didn't know the Prime Minister had his headquarters there, but I'm not surprised. They say it's the most secure location in all the Northern Elven Counties."

They crossed the river at the stepping stones and headed southeast along the edge of the blue pine forest. Twig wandered off among the trees.

"When I was little," said Alfur, "my grandmother used to recite a rhyme about the Caves of Kismet. By the way, I know I'm still little, so don't even bother saying it."

"Do you remember the rhyme?"

Alfur lowered his voice to a doom-laden whisper and began to chant:

> *"You want to get to the Caves of Kismet?*
> *You'll have to face three terrible tests:*
> *the Test of Courage, the Test of Skill,*
> *and the Test of Exceptional Braininess.*
> *What happens if you fail a test?*
> *Prepare yourself for certain death!"*

"Your grandmother sounds like a bundle of laughs," muttered Hilda.

"She was a wonderful woman," said Alfur. "Turn left here."

A narrow path led up a steep slope through the trees. It was overgrown with blue pine branches and Hilda had to use both arms to push the branches aside. She kept walking into spiderwebs, which clung to her face and made her wince in disgust.

Hilda had never been to the Great Waterfall before and she was beginning to feel nervous. "Alfur," she whispered. "Those tests you mentioned. Are you sure there isn't a test of rock sketching? Or crumpet toasting? Or Dragon Panic strategy?"

"Granny didn't mention any of those," said Alfur. "But you never know," he added kindly.

As they emerged from the forest onto a windblown hillside, something small and furry flew through the air and slammed into Hilda, knocking her off her feet.

She sat up and looked around to see what had hit her. Beside her on the ground lay a nut-brown rabbit with big dazed eyes.

"Aw, look," she said. "It's a cute little bunny rabbit."

"It's not just a rabbit," said Alfur.

"Hello, Bunny," said Hilda. "Are you all right?"

"It's not just a rabbit," said Alfur.

"You took a real tumble, didn't you, Bunny? Let me help you up."

"It's not just a rabbit," said Alfur.

"Well, what would you call it?" asked Hilda.

"I'd call it a Beast of the Light Brigade," said Alfur. "May I suggest you turn your head to the left."

Hilda looked left up the hill and let out a startled yelp. Charging towards her down the hill was a cavalry of rabbits, galloping and snarling and kicking up clods of earth and moss as they thundered onwards. Some of the rabbits were being ridden by elves in full battle armor.

"The Light Brigade is the Prime Minister's private cavalry," said Alfur. "They ride wild beasts into combat."

"Tally-ho!" cried the commander elf at the front of the brigade. "Implement Giant-Girl-Attack Maneuvers!"

Hilda noticed that many of the mounted elves were whirling slingshots around their heads.

"Fire at will!" bellowed the cavalry commander.

A tiny pebble whizzed past Hilda's head, then another and another.

"Now might be a good time to run away," suggested Alfur.

Hilda gritted her teeth. "I'm not running away," she said. "I'm going to the Caves of

69

Kismet. I'm going to save my home if it's the last thing I do."

"It will be," muttered Alfur.

Hilda dropped to a crouch and raised an arm to protect her face. Pebbles to right of her, pebbles to left of her, pebbles behind her volleyed and clattered.

The first rank of rabbits was almost upon her. Hilda dropped to the ground and rolled to avoid the thundering paws, but the rest of the cavalry charged right into her, knocking the breath clean out of her. The next thing she knew she was surrounded on all sides, being butted and rammed by bucktoothed bunnies. There were hundreds of them.

"Get off me!" panted Hilda. "Get off! Get off!"

Out of a nearby bush leaped a blur of white fur. It landed in the middle of the fray, growling and snarling savagely.

"Twig!" cried Hilda.

Six hundred bunnies were no match for one wild

deer fox. They scattered in terror, bucking their riders off their backs in their hurry to get away from those snapping teeth and jabbing antlers.

"Retreat!" cried the elf commander as he landed on the grass on his bottom. "Implement Giant-Girl-Retreat Maneuvers!"

The rabbits galloped off down the hill. Dismayed elf riders fled after them. The Light Brigade disappeared into the trees as suddenly as it had arrived.

"Thank you, Twig!" cried Hilda. "You're the bravest, most loyal friend an adventurer could hope for!"

"You were pretty brave yourself," whispered Alfur. "In fact, I think you just passed the Test of Courage."

8

Hilda, Alfur, and Twig journeyed on up the winding path that led to the Caves of Kismet. The path came to an end on a rocky plateau beside a waterfall. Thousands of gallons of water plunged past them into the fjord below.

"Where now?" asked Hilda.

"The path continues right there in front of you," said Alfur. "Look, it leads along the rock face and behind the waterfall."

Hilda looked and saw a narrow ledge no more than about an inch wide. "That's not a path," she said.

"It's an elf path," said Alfur. "I could walk along it easily."

"That's because your shoes are a hundred times smaller than mine," said Hilda. "Seriously, Alfur, how am I supposed to walk along that ledge?"

"There's no shame in failure," said Alfur. "If we turn back now, we'll be home in time for lunch."

"I'm not turning back," said Hilda. "I'm going to see the elf Prime Minister."

"*O-kaaay,*" said Alfur. "In that case, could you set me down? I'd rather not be in your ear when you fall off that ledge and plummet a thousand elf yards onto the rocks below."

"Fine." Hilda cupped her hand to her ear and lowered the elf to the ground. "I'll go first and you walk behind me, Alfur. Twig, you stay here and keep watch."

Hilda put down her adventuring satchel and

removed her boots and socks. She took a deep breath and stepped off the plateau onto the narrow ledge. The rock felt cold and slippery beneath her feet, worn smooth by many centuries of falling water. She stood on the tips of her toes, pressed her body against the cool rock face, and began to edge sideways, trying not to look down.

Twig followed behind her, lifting his nimble hooves one by one and placing them carefully on the narrow, slippery ledge. In all the time Hilda had known Twig, he had never obeyed a "stay" command. He was her friend, after all, not her pet.

Alfur brought up the rear, shaking his head. "You're going to slip!" he shouted.

"I'm not," said Hilda.

"You are!" shouted Alfur.

"I'm not," said Hilda through gritted teeth. "I'm not going to slip, I'm not going to slide, and I'm not going to fall, so there!"

So saying, she tossed her head confidently— and fell off the ledge!

Alfur shouted. Twig barked. Hilda's fingernails scrabbled helplessly at the smooth rock. As she slithered down the sheer rock face, she flung a desperate arm towards the plateau and managed to grab a tuft of scurvygrass.

The scurvygrass roots groaned and tore as they took Hilda's weight. With her legs flailing in thin air, she reached up, grabbed the edge of the plateau with her fingertips and hauled herself back up onto solid rock, trembling all over.

Twig and Alfur edged back along the ledge and ran to Hilda's side. Twig nudged her lovingly with his antlers. Alfur scowled at her as if to say, *I told you so.*

Hilda sat on the plateau and stared at the mass of falling water plummeting past her. "It's impossible," she gasped. "That ledge is as slippery as glass."

"You're in shock," said Alfur. "You should eat something."

Hilda reached into her adventuring satchel and

felt around for a cucumber sandwich. Her fingers touched something dry and sticky.

"Ew!" she exclaimed. "What's that?"

It was her sketchbook. She had not had time to clean it since yesterday's adventure, and the troll drool had dried into a sticky mess all over the cover of the book.

Hilda had an idea. She took out the book and started smearing the gluey saliva all over her hands, knees, and toes.

"What is that stuff?" said Alfur.

"You don't want to know," replied Hilda.

When she had finished, she stood up, took a deep breath, and stepped once more onto the slippery elf ledge. Pressing her knees, chest, and forehead against the rock, she shuffled along it on the tips of her toes.

"You're doing great!" shouted Alfur, springing up and settling himself back in her ear.

With the gummy troll spit on her hands and feet, Hilda did not slip as she squeezed between the rock face and the curtain of falling water behind her.

"Not far now," said Alfur.

Hilda felt sick with fear and her tiptoes ached from carrying her weight. But the path was getting wider and soon she was able to place her feet side by side and walk along more comfortably. At last she found herself on a wide shelf of rock behind the waterfall. Right in front of her were two dark cave openings.

Twig joined her on the rocky shelf. "The Caves of Kismet!" cried Alfur in her ear. "You've done it! You've passed the Test of Skill!"

"Indeed she has!" cried another voice. "But now she must face the Test of Exceptional Braininess, and judging by the look of her, I don't think she stands a chance."

"Hey," said Hilda. "I'm right here, you know." She looked down and saw an elf dressed as a jester. He wore long curly shoes and a tricorn hat with jingly bells.

"Two caves," said the elf. "One to your left, one to your right. The elf Prime Minister in one, a man-eating troll in the other. You make your choice, you meet your destiny."

Hilda stared down at the jester elf, then up at the dark cave entrances. "I don't believe there's a troll in either of these caves," said Hilda. "What would it find to eat in there?"

"Sometimes a woff strays into its cave," said the jester. "But mostly it eats travelers who make the wrong choice."

"And why doesn't it eat you?"

The jester grinned and pointed at the bells in his hat.

"OK," said Hilda. "I believe you now."

"Two water spirits guard the entrances," continued the jester. "One guards the left cave, one guards the right. To help you make your choice, you may ask ONE spirit ONE question."

"Easy," said Hilda. "I'll just ask which cave the Prime Minister is in."

"Not so fast," said the jester. "There is something else you should know. One spirit always tells the truth. The other always lies."

The falling water behind Hilda bulged and bubbled on either side of her, and two pairs of watery eyes appeared. Twig growled and backed away.

"The spirits look exactly the same," said Hilda. "How do I know which one is the liar?"

"You don't!" cackled the jester. "How I love this job! Now, enough of the talking. Ask your question and make your choice."

9

Twig growled. Alfur sighed. Hilda scratched her head.

"I know," she said at last. "I'll ask one of the spirits what color my hair is. If it answers blue, I'll know it's the truth-teller. If it answers anything else, I'll know it's the liar."

"So what?" said Alfur. "You still won't know which cave the Prime Minister is in, and you'll have used up your only question."

Hilda groaned in frustration. "Ow, my brain is hurting. Can't you just tell me, Alfur?"

"No," said Alfur. "I have never been exceptionally brainy."

"I thought you were a writer."

"Exactly," said Alfur.

"What about you, Twig?"

But Twig was no help either. He looked from the caves to the spirits, to caves to spirits, to caves to spirits so fast he ended up getting dizzy and falling over sideways.

Hilda groaned again. The brainiest person she knew was probably her mom. Even the Wood Man was pretty brainy. What would he say? she wondered.

"Wait, that's it!" Hilda turned to face the water spirit on her left. "Here's my question," she said. "If I asked the *other* spirit whether the Prime Minister is in *this* cave, *what would they say?*"

There followed a moment of silence and then a watery voice came from the spirit. "They . . . would . . . say . . . no."

"Aha!" said Hilda. "There are two possibilities

here. FIRST POSSIBILITY, you are the liar, in which case you're lying when you say the other spirit would say "no." So they wouldn't say "no," they would say "YES, the Prime Minister IS in this cave." And if you're the liar then they're the truth-teller and I can totally trust their "yes." SECOND POSSIBILITY, you are the truth-teller, in which case you are telling the truth about the other spirit saying "no." But if you're the truth-teller, they're the liar, so their "no" is itself a lie. Either way, the truth is the same. THE PRIME MINISTER IS IN THIS CAVE."

"In you go, then," said the jester.

Hilda ventured forwards into the darkness, followed by Alfur and Twig.

"Excuse me," said Alfur, clambering up into her ear again. "I didn't understand a word you just said. Would you mind telling me how sure you are that you've made the right choice? On a scale of, say, one to ten."

"Seven," said Hilda.

"That's what I was afraid of," muttered Alfur.

As Hilda moved forward, she bumped into a thick wooden door, which creaked open to reveal a beautiful cavern flooded with light. A dozen suited elves sat at a small rock table in the middle of the cavern.

"Aaargh!" cried the elves. "It's the giant girl!"

Twig heard the elves but could not see them. He dashed excitedly around the cavern and the suited elves dashed to and fro to avoid him.

"Twig, calm down!" shouted Hilda. "I come in peace," she added quietly. "Which one of you is the Prime Minister?"

An elf with a pointy chin climbed up onto the table. "I am the Prime Minister," he said. "What do you want, giant girl?"

"I want to stay in my house," said Hilda.

"Impossible," said the Prime Minister.

"Why?" cried Hilda. "What harm have I ever done to you?"

The Prime Minister spread his arms wide.

"You keep stepping on us!"

"That doesn't hurt you," said Hilda. "Last night I saw Twig's leg go right through a house without causing any damage."

"Yes, but look at it from our point of view. Imagine how traumatic it is having a giant foot come through the ceiling. And imagine how hard it is to get babies to sleep when two giants are chatting nearby."

Hilda looked at it from their point of view. For the first time, she stopped thinking about her own problems and she started imagining what it must be like to live in the shadow of giants, having to cope with deafening noise and bright lights and enormous feet clomping to and fro. The more she imagined it, the less angry she felt. In fact, she began to feel a little bit sorry.

"Forgive us," she said in a small voice. "We had no idea we were upsetting anyone. But now you've told us, we can try to change. We'll turn our lights off earlier and keep our voices down. And I'll get

Mom to sign the forms. If she can see you, she won't step on you any more."

The Prime Minister shook his head. "It's not as simple as that. For as long as anyone can remember, the occupants of your house have been considered enemies of the King. We've been at war with you for generations. It's just that no one has ever bothered to do anything about it, until me. I'm afraid that fixing the situation at this point is, er . . . "

"Out of your hands?" said Hilda.

"That's right." The Prime Minister held up his stubby arms. "And I don't even have hands."

Hilda stared at him. "You're saying that the only way I can save my home is to sign a peace treaty with the Elf King?"

"Exactly." The Prime Minister beamed.

"And where can I find the King?"

"I can't tell you."

"WHAT?!"

"I've signed a secrecy form promising not to

tell any non-elf the location of the King's castle. It's one of those forms that every elf signs as soon as they are old enough to write their name. Sorry about that."

10

That evening Hilda ate her stew and rowanberries with a heavy heart. She did not ask for a second helping. She did not ask Mom to play Dragon Panic or to toast marshmallows in front of the fire. She did not even want to flop on the sofa and read CAVES AND THEIR UNFRIENDLY OCCUPANTS. All she wanted to do was go to bed.

She had a bath, put on her pajamas and got into bed. Twig lay down on her feet and Mom

came into her bedroom to tuck her in and
say goodnight.

"Traumatic day?" asked Mom.

"Yes," said Hilda in a small voice. "I tried to fix
our problem with the elves, but it's impossible."

Mom came and sat on the edge of the bed. "It's
strange hearing you say that word."

Hilda scratched her head. "Elves?"

"No. *Impossible.* You hardly ever say
something's impossible."

"Get used to it." Hilda scratched her head
again.

"You're scratching a lot," said Mom. "Come
here and let me check your head."

Hilda leaned forward to let Mom explore her
hair. Mom picked up a comb and sketchbook and
started combing Hilda's hair over a blank page.
Tiny orange specks fell out onto the paper.

"Have I got nits?" Hilda asked.

"No," said Mom. "*Nittens.*"

Hilda grabbed her magnifying glass and

examined one of the specks. It looked like a minuscule version of Angelina, the elf mayor's cat. She remembered how Angelina had looked much thinner after hiding in her hair.

Mom continued to comb Hilda's hair in silence, and then she spoke again, a little too brightly. "I've been thinking, Hilda. We haven't been to Trolberg for ages. Let's go there tomorrow, just for the day."

"Mom, please."

"Just for the day," repeated Mom with a big fake smile. "Just to have a look around."

Mom poured the nittens into a tiny box on Hilda's bedside table. She kissed Hilda on the forehead, tucked her in, and left the room.

As soon as Mom was gone, Alfur jumped off the pile of books on Hilda's bedside table and peered into the nittens box. "I should probably take these to Angelina," he said.

"Yes, you should," said Hilda. "And don't bother coming back, unless you're going to tell me where the King's castle is."

Alfur shook his head. "You know I can't do that," he said. "I signed the secrecy form, just like everyone else. I'm not allowed to breathe a word to any non-elf about the location of the King's castle."

"Forms, forms, forms," Hilda said. "That's all you elves care about, isn't it?"

"Yes," said Alfur. "I mean, no. I mean, you can't pretend forms aren't important."

"And what about friendship?" Hilda cried. "Does that count for anything in your ridiculous, paper-filled little world?"

She switched off her bedside lamp and pulled her blankets violently up over her head, causing Twig to wake with a start and jump down off the bed.

Hilda tried to sleep. She closed her eyes and imagined water spirits gliding under a bridge. That usually made her doze off, but not tonight.

She could not stop thinking about her failure
with the elves and about Mom's plan to visit
Trolberg tomorrow.

Just to have a look around. Ha! To look at
houses, more like, and to sign Hilda up for a local
school. Hilda's eyes filled with tears.

The grandfather clock down in the hall chimed
twelve. And then there was another sound, a gentle
tapping on the window.

Hilda pushed back the covers and flicked on the
light. Twig was standing on the windowsill, pawing
at the glass.

"What is it, boy? What can you see?"

Hilda went to the window and gazed out.
The moon was high in the sky, shining down on
a thousand miniature houses. To the north loomed
Bobblehat Mountain, its lofty peak covered in
snow. To the east the river wound its way towards
Trolberg.

Twig scrabbled at the window. His neck fur
stood on end and his small black eyes were staring

up at the sky above Bobblehat Mountain, where a colossal head and shoulders blotted out the stars.

Hilda pressed her nose to the window. "It's the giant," she whispered. "The giant that comes at midnight."

The midnight giant turned its head slowly from side to side as if looking for something. Then it glanced down at Hilda's house and froze.

Hilda gazed up at the giant.

The giant gazed down at Hilda.

This time Hilda did not call for Mom. She just stood there with her hands flat against the windowpane. A great calm descended on her and the beating of her heart quieted to a peaceful thud. Her tears dried slowly on her cheeks.

The giant's eyes shimmered in the moonlight. It heaved a sigh, turned away slowly, and lumbered off into the darkness.

"Don't go," said Hilda. She undid the latch and threw her window wide open. "Please stay!" she shouted, but the giant had already disappeared.

11

The next morning Hilda sat in the car watching the countryside roll past. Sheep grazed. The river babbled. Blue pine branches waved in the fall breeze. There on the left was a steep hill that Hilda loved to roll down on her side. Here on the right was the biggest rowanberry bush in the whole valley and a patch of long grass perfect for making grass trumpets.

So many memories. So many things she would never do again.

Far away to the East, a forest giant blundered among the trees. Hilda had never thought of forest giants as small, but now she realized how tiny they were compared to last night's visitor. For the hundredth time that day, she thought about the midnight giant. Why did it keep coming to the valley? What was it waiting for? Why did it look so sad?

It was hard to think with Mom talking so much. She had hardly stopped chattering since they left the house an hour ago, going on and on about her own childhood in Trolberg and her weekend visits to her grandparents in the countryside.

"Perhaps we could do the same thing," Mom was saying as they drove over the bridge. "Live in Trolberg most of the time and visit the countryside some weekends. What do you think, Hilda?"

"Sounds great," said Hilda. "Except for the living in Trolberg part."

The River Björg was still on their right but it was wider now and slower. Up ahead Hilda saw the towering twin peaks of Mount Hár and Mount Halldór. Between the two mountains stood a high brick wall.

"You know why Trolberg has such tall city walls, don't you?" said Mom.

"To stop people escaping?"

"No!" Mom laughed. "To keep them safe from trolls. Trolberg was built smack dab in the middle of troll territory."

"I see," said Hilda. "So what you're saying is that we humans kicked the trolls out of their homeland just like the elves are kicking us out of our house."

"It happened a long time ago," Mom sighed. "Please don't be difficult today, Hilda."

They drove beneath a gigantic arch with the words WELCOME TO TROLBERG painted on it. Two bell towers stood either side of the arch like prison watchtowers. Hilda guessed that the bell towers were meant to keep the trolls away from the city. She had seen for herself how much trolls hated the sound of bells.

Hilda wound down the window and poked her head out to inspect the city. It was even grimmer than she remembered it: a town square full of wretched pigeons, a bare concrete schoolyard surrounded by a wire fence, and a maze of dirty streets lined with dirty houses.

"All right, we've seen the city," said Hilda. "Can we go home now?"

"No," said Mom. "I have a whole list of places I want us to look at together, starting with the Edmund Ahlberg School. Don't look so gloomy, Hilda. You never know, you might like it here."

They spent the whole day in Trolberg, traipsing to and fro and trudging up and down stairs to inspect miserable two-bedroom apartments. The streets all looked the same to Hilda, and so did the houses, which stood squashed up next to each other in long rows. Not at all like their home in the country, where level wilderness stretched far away to distant snowcapped mountains.

Mom seemed different in the city too.
She swung her arms fast as she walked and she
kept looking at her watch. It was like she was
turning into a Trolberg businesswoman right
before Hilda's eyes.

The absolute worst thing about Trolberg was
the bells. It had been so long since Hilda last
visited Trolberg that she had forgotten how many
bell towers there were, not just along the city walls
but all over the city. The frequent ringing and
bonging and dinging and donging made Hilda
jump in fright and clap her hands to her ears, and
when she and Mom returned home in the car that
night, her ears were still ringing.

"Please don't make us move, Mom," Hilda
pleaded as they drove out into the countryside.

"It will be good for you, Hilda. You'll be able
to make some friends at last."

"I have friends already."

"I'm talking about human friends."

"I don't want human friends! And I don't want to live in Trolberg. There's nothing to draw, there's nowhere to explore, the whole city smells of car fumes, and I didn't see a single rowanberry bush all day."

"Hilda, we don't have a choice."

"Yes, and the reason we don't have a choice is because you're not DOING anything. Me, I've been out negotiating with mayors and dodging rabbits and smearing troll spit on my feet, trying my best to fix things with the elves. And what have you been doing? Nothing! You know what I think, Mom? I think you *want* to move. I think you've been planning it for ages!"

"You're wrong, Hilda." Mom's voice shook with strong emotion. "And if you can't say anything nice, don't say anything at all."

"Fine by me!" snapped Hilda.

They drove the rest of the way home in heavy silence and did not speak to each other for the rest of the day.

12

That night Hilda sat by the window with Twig, waiting for the midnight giant. She was not sure why she found its presence so comforting. Perhaps it was its immense size, which somehow made her problems feel smaller, or perhaps it was the tears that shimmered in its eyes, as if it understood her pain. She wished she could talk to it and ask it for advice.

At five minutes to midnight a flicker of movement made her heart leap. But it was not the midnight giant. It was a flock of woffs migrating.

Woff migration was a common event in the Björg valley. Every few days long lines of woffs would come flying up the valley in search of woff knows what, their big eyes peering into the darkness ahead of them and their tails flickering from side to side as they flew.

Downstairs in the hall the grandfather clock began to chime.

One . . . *two* . . . *three* . . . Hilda stared into the darkness . . .

Four . . . *five* . . . *six* . . . Twig's ears pricked up and he started to paw the windowpane . . .

Seven . . . *eight* . . . *nine* . . . Hilda fixed her eyes on the peak of Bobblehat Mountain . . .

Ten . . . *eleven* . . . *twelve*. Perhaps the midnight giant was not going to come tonight . . .

Hilda looked at Twig. He was standing on his hind legs, craning his neck as if trying to see behind the mountain. "What is it, boy?" she murmured, opening the window and leaning out.

Then she saw it. A strange bulge on the mountainside, a bulge that looked for all the world like a giant's elbow sticking out.

"It's over there!" cried Hilda. "It's sitting behind Bobblehat Mountain! Right, I'm going to talk to it."

She scrambled out onto the roof and made her way to the edge. The wind blew cold, making her gasp and shiver. "Hello!" she cried, her voice echoing back to her off the mountainside. "I'm Hilda! What's your name?"

Ever so slowly the midnight giant got to its feet. Its head and shoulders loomed over the top of the mountain as before. It glanced at Hilda and let out a great sigh that made all the fir trees on the mountainside shudder.

And then it turned to leave.

"No, you don't!" cried Hilda. "There's no way I'm letting you get away this time!"

She got up and started running along the roof towards the midnight giant, spreading her arms wide for better balance. Out of the corner of her eye she could see the tail end of the woff formation approaching. The very last woff was about to fly past the edge of the roof.

Hilda sped up to match the speed of the woff and then, without even thinking about what she was doing, she launched herself off the roof, through the air, and onto the woff.

The startled woff went wild, soaring and bucking, snuffling and clucking. Hilda wrapped her legs under the belly of the beast and clung onto its neck fur for dear life, steering north towards the midnight giant.

The midnight giant lumbered away with gigantic steps, making immense footprints like the one Hilda had seen in the meadow. The giant was fast, but Hilda's woff was faster. It shot through the air like a pebble from an elf's slingshot, higher and higher into the clouds, closer and closer to the striding giant. Hilda whooped and held on tight.

Thick clouds were all around her, but suddenly they parted and Hilda saw the head of the midnight giant right below her.

"Thanks for the ride, Woffie!" she shouted. "One, two, three, geronimooooooo!"

She dropped off the woff and fell down, down, down onto the midnight giant's head. Its fur was thick and dark like scurvygrass and it had a pleasant, chalky smell.

"Hi!" she cried.

The giant kept moving. It seemed not to have heard.

Hilda climbed down the side of the giant's head and found a cavernous earhole in amongst the dark fur.

"Excuse me, sir!" she called, wriggling into the earhole.

The giant stopped walking. "Who are you?" it said, and its voice was like sad thunder.

"I'm the girl from the house over there,"

gabbled Hilda.

"It's nice to meet you at last. I'm a big fan of yours. People must tell you this all the time, but you're so big! I've never seen anyone as big as you. You're huge-mungous. Tell me, why do you keep coming here at midnight?"

The giant was silent for a long time before answering. "I arranged to meet someone," it said at last.

"Who?" asked Hilda, curious.

"An old friend."

"Are you sure you have the right place?"

The giant turned its head to scan the landscape. Nestled on the ridge of the giant's inner ear, Hilda gazed out across the moonlit valley— the forests, the river, and the distant mountains she loved so much.

"I remember the positions of the stars," said the giant, "and the smell of thyme and rowanberries. The hills have shifted a little. And your house is new. But yes, this is the place."

114

"So why has your friend not come?"

"I don't know." The giant moved off again, stalking back towards Bobblehat Mountain. "The meeting was arranged a long, long time ago. We said we would meet here at midnight. Maybe I got the date wrong."

"You don't seem like the kind of person to forget an important date," said Hilda. "I'm sorry to say this, but I don't think your friend is coming."

"Not coming." The midnight giant pondered Hilda's words. "Perhaps you're right. Perhaps she's gone, just like the others."

"She? Who is she? Tell me about her."

The giant did not reply. It came to a stop next to Hilda's house and raised its hand to its ear. It lowered her down and let her slide off its finger onto the roof of her house.

"Sorry," Hilda called. "I didn't mean to ask so many questions. But you seemed so sad, and I've been feeling sad as well, and I just thought—"

"Goodbye, little girl," said the giant.
"Thank you for the chat."

With that, it straightened up and trudged
off into the night.

13

The next day Hilda went with Twig to visit the Wood Man's house in the middle of the Great Forest. The house was a beautiful two-story cabin made of pine and walnut wood, built around the base of an enormous oak tree. As Hilda and Twig approached the cabin they heard smooth jazz music from within.

The Wood Man opened the door to Hilda's knock. His wooden face was not able to show much expression, but his eyes did get a little wider and his mouth a little rounder.

"How do you know where I live?" he said.

"I've been exploring this valley my whole life," said Hilda. "Aren't you going to ask me in?"

"No."

Hilda shrugged. "I'll come in anyway."

The inside of the Wood Man's house was beautiful. It had cream-white floorboards, a gleaming piano, and a cosy wood-burning stove. Every wall was lined with bookshelves.

"Tea?" asked the Wood Man, offering Hilda a mug of soily water with sticks in it.

"I'm afraid I've got no time for tea," said Hilda. "I need to borrow one of your books."

"Do I look like a librarian?" said the Wood Man.

Hilda sighed. "No, you don't. But I noticed the other day that you were reading a book about giants. I wondered if I could have a look at it."

The Wood Man went to the corner of the room. He climbed a stepladder and started hunting for his book on giants. Twig jumped onto the piano

and pranced along it *plinkety-plinkety-plonkety-plunk* all the way down to the booming low notes.

"Here it is," said the Wood Man. He pulled a hefty book off the top shelf and passed it down to Hilda.

THINGS WITH BIG FEET:
A Guide to Every Giant You've Ever Seen,
as Well as Some You Haven't
by Sigrid Renberg

"Perfect," said Hilda. She sat down in a basket chair and ran her finger down the index of the book. "Forest giants, snow giants, horse giants . . . Ah, here we are—ancient giants."

Hilda turned to the right page, pushed her hair behind her ear, and started to read.

When the world was young, ancient giants lived in the valleys of the North. They were taller than mountains and could live for many thousands of years. One giant always sat atop the tallest mountain, a long-forgotten peak in the frozen lands. He sat there gazing into the black, guarding the Earth from anything that might threaten from above. Any young giant could be chosen as the Guardian, a duty that could last thousands of years.

Hilda turned the page and her eye fell on a picture of the midnight giant. "That's him!" she cried. "It says here that his name is Jørgen. It says he was the last of the ancient giants to serve as Guardian."

Hilda frowned as she continued to read.

Everything changed when human beings appeared in the valleys of the North. They built towns which the ancient giants would accidentally step on. This led to arguments and fights. When the ancient giants realized that the world had

123

become too small for them, they upped and left.
No one knows where they went. Some say they
just jumped as high as they could and drifted off
into space.

"Poor Jørgen!" cried Hilda. "The ancient giants
all left without him. He's been sitting on some
frozen mountaintop all on his own for thousands
of years, keeping watch, and no one told him that
everyone else was gone! His friend was supposed
to meet him but she's gone too.
He's all on his own, poor guy."

The Wood Man looked at her with empty eyes.
"Have you finished?"

"Finished what?"

"Reading. Talking. Being in my house."

"Sure." Hilda closed book and stood up.
"Thanks for showing me the book, Wood Man.
Come on, Twig. Last one home is a rotten
woff egg!"

An hour and a half later, Hilda barged in through the front door of her house and kicked off her red rubber boots. The house was toasty warm and a divine aroma of ginger, nutmeg, and caraway seeds wafted over her. Only one thing was different. Mom was not at her desk, nor in the kitchen.

Hilda went upstairs, followed by Twig. Mom was in Hilda's bedroom, pulling clothes out of the wardrobe and putting them in a suitcase.

"What are you doing?" cried Hilda.

"Packing." Mom dropped an armful of wool sweaters into a suitcase. "I'm afraid another of those tiny letters arrived. Same message as usual, except this time it has the words FINAL WARNING stamped all over it in red ink."

"We can't let them bully us!" cried Hilda, stamping her foot. "Hey, I have an idea. We'll make the house into a castle. I'll dig a moat! And if they find a way in, I'll use the broom again, like I did before."

"I'm sorry, Hilda." Mom snapped the suitcase shut and plonked it down on the floor. "I'm packing up the house. We're moving to Trolberg tomorrow."

Mom went downstairs and Hilda slumped down at her desk with her head in her hands. Twig came and curled up at her feet.

Her sketchbook lay in front of her on the desk, open at her map of the valley. She gazed down at Boot Mountain, Bobblehat Mountain, the river, the Great Forest, and the Blue Pine Forest. Places she had spent her childhood exploring. Places she might never see again . . .

Hilda started to cry. Big fat tears rolled down her cheeks and dropped onto the map.

"Please don't cry," said a little voice.

Hilda looked down at Twig, amazed. She didn't know he could talk. He had certainly never spoken before.

"Over here," said the voice.

Hilda wiped her eyes and saw Alfur the elf

sitting on a pencil sharpener. "Oh, it's you," she said.

Alfur grinned at her. "You thought the deer fox spoke, didn't you?"

"Of course not," Hilda lied. "And for your information, this is my room so I'll cry if I want to. You would cry too, if you had to leave your home."

"I'm just saying, I don't like seeing you sad," Alfur mumbled.

"Yes, you do," Hilda snapped. "Otherwise you'd have told me where the King lives."

"Hey, that's not fair!" Alfur hopped off the pencil sharpener and walked towards her. "It's out of my hands. I signed the secrecy form. There's no way I can tell you the location of the King."

"Whatever," Hilda muttered.

"I can't say a word," said Alfur, stepping onto the map.

"Leave me alone, then," said Hilda. "Go on, scram!"

"Not a single word," repeated Alfur. He was

behaving very oddly, jumping up and down on Hilda's map. "I can't say anything at all. I refuse to speak. I am silent on the matter. Do you understand?"

Hilda sat back and stared at the little elf, who seemed to have completely lost his mind, dancing up and down on the spot, pointing at his shoes.

"Do you understand?" Alfur repeated. "Do you understand?"

Hilda looked at the elf's shoes, which were tap dancing on the picture of Bobblehat Mountain, right next to the picture of her house. A smile spread slowly across her face.

"I understand," she said, reaching for her warmest coat and scarf. "Alfur, you dear little creature! How would you like to come for a walk with me?"

14

Bobblehat Mountain was right next to Hilda's house. She had explored it many times before, but only on the grassy slopes, never above the snowline.

Beware of climbing above the snowline, Mom had always told her. *It's dangerous. There are deep holes you can fall into. There are weather spirits. And worst of all, there is the risk of an avalanche.*

Hilda knew what an avalanche was—a huge wave of snow thundering down a mountainside, sweeping away everything in its path. The thought of it terrified her.

But the thought of moving to Trolberg terrified her even more.

With her adventuring satchel on her back, Twig by her side, and Alfur in her ear, she set off up the grassy slopes of Bobblehat Mountain, determined to reach the Elf King's castle on the snowy mountain peak.

As soon as they passed the snowline the mountain got steeper and more difficult to climb. Hilda pulled her yellow scarf tight around her neck and picked up a birch branch to use as a walking stick. On every step Hilda poked the stick into the snow in front of her to make sure there were no hidden holes. Snow crunched and squeaked

beneath her feet. Twig followed in her footsteps, lowering his head into the wind.

"Oh dear," said Alfur suddenly. "That weather spirit looks angry!"

"What weather spirit?"

A flurry of snow descended on Hilda, covering her head and shoulders.

"*That* weather spirit," said Alfur.

Hilda looked up and another flurry fell right into her eyes. There was a dark snow cloud directly above her head. To her left and right the weather was dry and sunny, but she and Alfur were trapped in their own personal blizzard. Twig darted to and fro, leaping into the air and snapping at the unruly spirit.

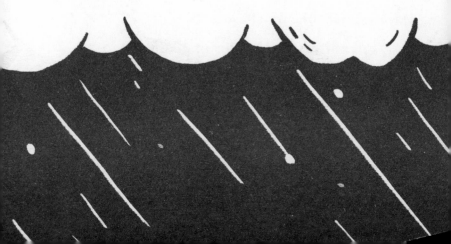

"Spirit, stop it!" cried Hilda. "You're being very annoying!"

"ANNOYING, AM I?!" roared the weather spirit, dumping a massive load of snow that knocked Hilda to her knees. "I'LL SHOW YOU ANNOYING!"

The snow piled up around Hilda. It was up to her thighs. It was up to her waist. It was up to her chest. It was up to her neck . . .

"Make friends with it!" cried Alfur. "Your mom is always saying how good you are at making friends with magical creatures. Make friends with it, quick, or it will bury us both!"

"Don't mind my elf!" Hilda called to the weather spirit. "He doesn't like mountain climbing. He'd rather take an elfevator!"

"I'm not your elf," Alfur muttered.

The weather spirit chuckled.

"My elf is a writer!" yelled Hilda. "He learned the elfabet at school!"

"I'm not your elf!" snapped Alfur.

The weather spirit sniggered. It was still snowing, but more lightly now.

"My elf has pockets full of gold!" shouted Hilda. "He's very welfy."

The weather spirit laughed again, and a slender ray of sunshine broke through the cloud.

"Enough of the elf jokes," protested Alfur.

"My elf loves baking," yelled Hilda, "but he can only make shortbread!"

"Tell me another," chortled the weather spirit.

"No, don't!" said Alfur.

"Here's a good one," shouted Hilda. "How many elves does it take to change a light bulb?"

"I don't know."

"A hundred!" yelled Hilda. "One to change the bulb, nine to stand on each other's shoulders and ninety to fill out the paperwork!"

The weather spirit roared with laughter. "Ninety to fill out the paperwork!" it echoed. "That's really very good. I'm going to go and tell my friends."

The spirit floated off as quickly as it had arrived. Twig lowered his antlers for Hilda to grab onto, and she heaved herself out of the snowdrift.

"Why did they all have to be elf jokes?" huffed Alfur.

"Sorry," said Hilda. "Those were the only ones that came to mind."

As she trudged on upwards, Hilda could feel melting snow trickling down the back of her neck. She shivered with cold and her legs felt tired and heavy. She stopped next to a silver birch tree and leaned against the trunk.

"How much further is it?" she panted.

"You know I can't tell you where the King's castle is," said Alfur, "but changing the subject, I think this lovely walk will last another four hours."

"Four hours!" Hilda bent over and put her hands on her knees. "I don't think I could walk for another four *minutes*."

Just then she heard a strange snuffling sound

above her head. She peered up into the silver birch tree and saw a line of yellow woffs sitting on a branch. They were snoring their heads off, regaining their energy before the next stage of their migration.

"Twig," Hilda whispered. "I can't take you with me on this next part of the journey. I'll see you later. I'll try not to be too long."

Hilda climbed the tree and edged along the woff branch. The loyal deer fox blinked his intelligent black eyes and growled softly.

"Excuse me." Alfur cleared his throat. "As long as I'm sitting in your ear, the least you can do is to share your plans with me. What exactly are you doing?"

"This," said Hilda, reaching out and grabbing the nearest woff by the scruff of its neck.

The woff woke up. Its big eyes bulged. It opened its mouth and gave a yelp of fright that echoed up and down the mountainside.

"Hold on tight, Alfur!" cried Hilda, and the

woff shot out of the tree as if its tail was on fire.

Hilda tugged gently on its fur to direct it up the mountainside. Up it went, faster and faster, past craggy rocks and mounds of snow.

"I feel woffsick," Alfur moaned. "This is why you should never fly without a permit."

"We're nearly at the summit!" yelled Hilda. "Let me know when you spot the King's c—

Aaaaaaargh!"

The woff sped up and looped the loop. Hilda lost her balance and slid off its back. As she fell, she reached up and grabbed the woff's tail with both hands, causing it to crash straight into a snowbank. BOOFFF*!*

Hilda lay on her back in the snow. She opened her eyes. "I'm OK," she said.

"No, you're not," said Alfur. "Neither of us are."

"Huh?" Hilda sat up. "What do you mean?"

"Listen," said Alfur.

Hilda listened. At first she heard nothing, and

then she detected a faint rumbling sound further up the mountain, getting louder and louder with every moment that passed.

"What's that?" she said.

"That," said Alfur, "is what we elves refer to as an avalanche. Although usually we say it more like this: AVALANCHE!!!"

The rumbling turned into a roar and Hilda saw a massive tidal wave of snow heading down the mountain straight towards her.

15

The avalanche thundered towards Hilda.
It looked like a great white wall, rearing higher
and higher into the sky and gathering speed
as it came.

Hilda turned and ran, but the avalanche was
faster. It was nearly upon her.

"May I suggest," said Alfur, "that you turn
your head to the right."

Hilda looked and saw what looked like the
dark mouth of a cave. She sprinted towards it,

stumbling over ice and rocks, and threw herself into the cave just as the avalanche struck. There was a deafening roar as thousands of tons of snow crashed past the mouth of the cave and down the mountainside.

Hilda lay on her back on the warm rocky floor. She opened her eyes. "I'm OK," she said.

"No, you're not," said Alfur. "Neither of us are."

"What is it?" she snapped. "What's wrong now?"

"This isn't a cave," said Alfur.

"What?"

"It's too warm," said Alfur.

"Nonsense," said Hilda, but now that she thought about it, the cave *was* strangely warm. It reminded her of last night, sitting in Jørgen's ear as the midnight giant strode along the valley looking for his friend. The friend that was supposed to be here, but wasn't.

Or is she? thought Hilda suddenly. If the cave

is an ear, then perhaps the mountain is not a mountain at all?

"Hello!" called Hilda. "Hellooooo!"

"HELLO?" A sleepy female voice rumbled through the mountain. "WHO'S THERE? REVEAL YOURSELF!"

"I'm right here!" cried Hilda.

"A voice in my head," said the female voice. "How strange."

Hilda stood up and went to the mouth of the cave. "Hey, I'm not just a voice in your head. I'm—"

The ground began to rumble beneath Hilda's feet. Rocks and stones and powdery snow tumbled off the mountainside. Hilda lost her footing and she plunged downwards, bouncing off boulders and rocky outcrops and ending up on a narrow ledge.

Hilda closed her eyes and hung on tight as the ledge, along with the entire mountainside, rose into the air as if being lifted on massive stilts.

The truth hit Hilda like an avalanche.

Bobblehat Mountain, the mountain that had stood next to her house since long before she was born, was not a mountain at all. And the summit of the mountain, the part that looked like a tiny bobble on a wool hat, was in fact a round head on a colossal triangular body.

Hilda opened her eyes and stared up at the giant's snow-covered hair and the massive shell-shaped earhole she had mistaken for a cave.

"You're an ancient giant!" yelled Hilda.

"Am I?" murmured the giant sleepily. "Yes, of course I am. Oh dear, how long have I been asleep?"

Hilda was about to answer when she noticed something above the giant's ear—a tiny red and white box perched on the edge of a high rock. Hilda squinted up at it, wondering what it was.

Alfur was the first to realize. "The castle!" he cried. "The Elf King's castle! And it's going to fall!"

Alfur was right. As the last tremors of the

earthquake died away, the castle teetered
and toppled and started to fall.

"It's going to smash on the rocks," Alfur
screamed. "It's going to be completely
comminuted!"

Hilda looked up at the falling castle, then down
to her right, where a deep drift of snow lay along
the giant's shoulder. Perhaps there was something

she could do, but she would only get one chance and her move would have to be absolutely perfect.

Without stopping to think about the danger to herself, Hilda took a run-up, launched herself off the ledge, grabbed the falling castle in midair, and landed in the soft snow, cradling the castle to her chest.

"Amazing!" cried Alfur. "You saved the King! You saved the castle!"

Hilda puffed out her cheeks. So far so good, but there was one more thing she knew she had to do. She slipped the castle into her adventuring satchel for safe keeping and scrambled up the female giant's face to perch on the edge of her ear once more.

"Excuse me!" Hilda shouted. "Are you looking for Jørgen?"

"Jørgen!" cried the female giant. "Yes! Have you seen him? Am I too late? I've waited for so long . . ."

"He's been coming every night at midnight!"

cried Hilda. "Why didn't you notice? I'm sorry, I'm afraid I told him not to wait any longer. I don't know where he's gone now . . . "

The female giant sighed. "The snow must have blocked my ears," she said.

A huge finger rose into the air, heading straight for the ear where Hilda stood.

"Careful with that finger!" cried Hilda. "Careful!"

It was too late. The finger reached into the ear, knocking Hilda aside and sending her plunging downwards once more, past the giant's chin and shoulder and chest, faster and faster, cold air whistling past her as she fell.

"I think this is the end for both of us," cried Alfur. "Nice knowing you, Hilda."

"You too!" shouted Hilda. "Sorry about those elf jokes!"

But in truth she was sorry about more than a few elf jokes. As Hilda fell through the air, the only face in her mind was the face of her mom. She felt so sorry about how mean she had been to Mom these last few days. More than anything she felt sorry that she would never again be able to tell Mom how much she loved her.

Hilda's hat flew off. Her sweater and scarf billowed and flapped, and the ground rushed up to meet her.

16

A vast midnight-colored hand swooped between Hilda and the ground, catching her neatly in the soft fur of its palm.

"Got you," said the midnight giant in a voice like happy thunder.

"Jørgen!" cried Hilda.

"Jørgen!" cried Alfur.

"JØRGEN!" cried the female giant.

The midnight giant put Hilda down on the ground and opened his arms to his friend. "You're here!" he cried, gathering her into a tight hug. "But how? Where were you on the nights that I

waited for you?"

"I was right here all along!" exclaimed the female giant, her voice muffled by Jørgen's fur.

"My love, things got complicated after you left. The little people came. Everyone was fed up and decided to leave, or hide. But I couldn't bear to leave without you. I came to the spot we arranged to meet, and I sat down and waited, and waited, and waited. I must have fallen asleep at some point."

Hilda listened with amazement. She imagined the sleeping giant's body becoming encrusted with rock, moss, and snow over thousands of years. By the time Jørgen finished his duty as Guardian and came back for her, his girlfriend would have looked like any other mountain.

"You waited for me for four thousand years," said Jørgen. "I'm so sorry."

"It's OK," said the female giant. "We're together. That's all that matters now."

The giant's words went right down into Hilda's

heart. She realized that she had spent so much time over the last few days thinking and worrying about losing her home, she had forgotten the thing that makes home home in the first place— the presence of the people you love. *It's OK. We're together. That's all that matters now.*

"Hello?" called a tiny voice from Hilda's adventuring satchel. "Is anybody there?"

"The King!" cried Alfur. "Quick, let him out."

Hilda unzipped the satchel and placed the castle carefully on the ground. A gate came up and a drawbridge came down and out of the castle stepped a regal-looking elf holding a scepter and a scroll.

"Young miss," he announced. "In light of recent events, I, the King, would like to declare an end to the conflict between you and my people. By saving my castle and everyone in it, you have shown yourself to be a person of honor. I will send a message to the Prime Minister immediately to inform him of the news. Now, if you'll just sign this peace treaty, we can make it official."

Hilda took the tiny scroll and signed it quickly. "So, we're no longer your enemies?" she asked.

"Not in the slightest," said the King.

"And we don't have to move?"

"Of course not," beamed the King. "You have as much right to live here as we do."

"Thank you!" Hilda cried. She looked over at her house with the checkered curtains in its windows and a plume of smoke curling from its little chimney. Her heart filled up with happiness.

As Hilda gazed at the house, the front door opened and out came Mom and Twig. Mom was carrying two heavy suitcases out to the car and it took her a moment to notice the two mountainous giants hugging each other. When she did, she went so weak at the knees she had to grab the car to steady herself. With her pale face and her mouth opening and closing silently, she looked like a very surprised catfish.

Hilda ran to Mom and squeezed her hard

around the waist. "I love you so much, Mom. I'm sorry I was angry with you."

Mom smiled weakly. "I love you too, Hilda. Now tell me, please, what on earth is happening here?"

"OK, it's like this." Hilda took a deep breath. "Bobblehat Mountain isn't a mountain—she's actually an ancient giant, and that furry black giant hugging her is called Jørgen, and the invisible red and white box over there is the Elf King's castle, and basically, well, the thing is . . . WE DON'T HAVE TO MOVE!!!!!!!!"

Mom looked at the spot where Hilda said the invisible castle was, and then went back to goggling up at the giants.

Twig jumped into Hilda's arms and she scratched the fur on the back of his neck.

"Let's walk and talk," the female giant said to Jørgen. "After four thousand years of sitting down I need to stretch my legs."

"Good idea," said Jørgen.

Off they strode, arm in arm, a perfect picture of Happy Ever After, spoiled only by the fact that Jørgen's very first step landed right on top of Hilda's house. Like a matchbox trodden on by a bear, the house and all its contents were completely flattened in an instant.

"Our house!" gasped Mom. "Our beautiful house!"

Hilda stared at the crushed house. For a few shocked seconds she felt nothing at all, but then her heart filled up with the words of the female giant.

"It's OK," Hilda whispered, slipping her hand into Mom's. "We're together. That's all that matters now."

Striding among the hills with his lady giant love, Jørgen did not even notice the destruction he had caused. The two giants came to a vast meadow of arctic poppies and there they linked their hands, bent their knees, and launched off into space.

17

Hilda and Mom stood hand in hand, looking
at the wreckage of their house—a tangle of planks,
logs, roof tiles, broken glass, and chimney bricks.

Hilda reached down and pulled a long
checkered rag out of the rubble. "Oh well," she
whispered. "You always said you didn't like
these curtains."

Mom made a strange sound somewhere
between a laugh and a sob.

Hilda squeezed her hand. She was about to say something else when she spotted two wooden legs poking out from the middle of the wreckage. At first she thought they were chair legs, but then she saw one of them twitch.

"The Wood Man!" she shrieked.

Hilda pulled her hand out of her mom's grip and set off, clambering over the planks and rubble to get to him. The wreckage shifted beneath her feet, making her stumble and trip, but at last she reached the wooden legs and pulled at them gently.

POP! Out of the ruins of the house the Wood Man emerged with the same bored, doleful expression as always. Hilda put an arm around his shoulders and used her scarf to wipe the dust out of his eyes.

"Are you OK?" she asked.

"I've lost my place," the Wood Man replied tonelessly.

"It was our place too," said Hilda.

"I mean, I've lost my place in this," said the Wood Man, holding up Hilda's copy of *CAVES AND THEIR UNFRIENDLY OCCUPANTS*. "I was in the middle of reading it when your house fell on top of me."

Hilda kept her arm around the Wood Man's shoulders and helped him back across the rubble to where Mom and Twig were standing. On the way she picked up a copper kettle and her sketchbook, which was now covered in dust as well as troll spit.

"Well done," said Mom. "But don't set foot on the wreckage again, Hilda. It's not safe."

It was late afternoon and the sun was low in the sky, slanting through the pine trees. Hilda and her mom spread the curtain on the grass like a picnic rug and they sat down to make a plan. After what had happened, it was clear they would have to move to Trolberg after all.

"Our apartment in Trolberg will be ready tomorrow," said Mom, "but I have no idea where we're going to sleep tonight. Any ideas, Hilda?"

Hilda thought about the Wood Man's beautiful pine and walnut cabin in the woods. She looked at him and raised her eyebrows. "Any ideas, Wood Man?"

"Yes," said the Wood Man.

"Well?"

"You have a tent, don't you?"

Luckily Hilda's camping gear was in one of the suitcases in the car. They pitched her tent between the bludbok tree and the catfish pond, well away from any elf houses. Hilda's mom built a fire and they used the copper kettle to make enormous mugs of hot chocolate. Twig lay nearby, his eyes half-closed, a picture of peace and relaxation.

"Our last night in the wilderness," said Hilda's mom, gazing up at the stars.

Hilda wrapped her hands around her mug to keep them warm. She would miss the countryside for sure, but sitting here under the stars she could not help feeling that she was on the edge of another grand adventure. Things had a habit of happening to her, wherever she was.

She felt a sudden tug on her earlobe. "What is it, Alfur?" she whispered.

"I was thinking," Alfur said. "Maybe I could come with you to Trolberg. We elves have always been interested in the world beyond this valley. If I came with you I could write reports about city life and send them back to my people here."

"Of course," said Hilda. "The more the merrier."

"There will be a mountain of paperwork, of course," Alfur said. "The elf passport application alone is two hundred and seventy pages."

"You'd better get started, then," smiled Hilda. "We'll see you back here at sunrise, ready for our new adventure."

Alfur climbed down Hilda's scarf and ran off into the darkness.

"Who were you talking to?" asked Mom.

"I'll tell you later," Hilda said. "But first I have

something very important to ask you."

"Go on."

"Did you pack the Dragon Panic board game, or did it get flattened?"

"I'm pretty sure it's in the suitcase."

Hilda grinned and flexed her fingers. "Then what are we waiting for?" she said. "I'll give you a three square head start and an extra healing potion in your kit bag, and I'll still wipe you off the board."

"Oh yeah?" Mom laughed and wagged her finger in the firelight.

"Yeah."

"Yeah?"

"Yeah!"

"Yeah?"

"YEAH!"

Mom threw herself on Hilda and started tickling her. Mother and daughter rolled around in the firelight, squawking with laughter, as if they did not have a care in the world.

Enjoyed *Hilda and the Hidden People*?
Then don't miss the second book in the series . . .

HILDA
AND THE GREAT PARADE

Hardback ISBN: 978-1-911171-45-4

With all new adventures from Hilda's move to Trolberg—
where she meets wild elves, fire-breathing dragons,
a mysterious talking raven, and even some new friends.

Can't wait to get your hands on it?
Here's a sneak peek just for you . . .

A clock ticked. A fly buzzed. Hard chalk squeaked on a dry chalkboard. Hunched on a wooden bench, a little girl with blue hair sat in the classroom with her cheek on her chin, gazing out of the window at the skyscrapers downtown.

"Hilda!" called Miss Hallgrim. "WHAT is so INTERESTING out there?"

Hilda blinked and turned to look at her teacher. Miss Hallgrim had a square jaw, stern eyes and a mass of white hair that made her look as if she was glaring out from the middle of a cloud.

"Interesting, Miss? Nothing, Miss," said Hilda.

Isn't that the truth? she thought. Nothing interesting going on out there and nothing interesting in here. Nothing interesting in all of Trolberg. Not like my old home in the wilderness, where there were mountains to climb, caves to explore, and all sorts of magical creatures to befriend . . .

"What was I SAYING, Hilda?" Miss Hallgrim demanded. She had an alarming habit of making her voice go suddenly loud and then quiet again.

"You were saying . . . " Hilda shielded her eyes and squinted sideways at her neighbor Frida's exercise book. One of the reasons that Frida was top of the class was that she took copious notes on everything Miss Hallgrim said. "You were saying that the Great Parade is three days from now. It is the most special day of the year in Trolberg and our class has been chosen to decorate a stoat for the parade."

The class sniggered. Hilda peered more closely at Frida's handwriting. "A float!" she cried, too late.

"Not a stoat, a float. Like a carnival float.

No one decorates stoats. That would be dumb.
They don't even stay still."

Laughter rang in Hilda's ears. Not kind laughter
but the sort of cruel, mocking laughter that she had
heard so many times in class these last two weeks.
Hilda's cheeks burned and she lowered her head
so that her blue hair fell in curtains on both sides
of her face.

"SILENCE," said Miss Hallgrim frostily.
"Hilda is correct, we are going to decorate a FLOAT.
In addition, we will prepare an EXHIBITION for your
parents to come and look at. You will work together
in groups of three to collect FASCINATING objects on
the theme of"—she turned to write on the board—
"WONDERFUL TROLBERG."

Hilda snorted. She didn't mean to snort. The
sound burst out of her nose all by itself as soon as
she heard Miss Hallgrim say "Wonderful Trolberg."
If ever there were two words that didn't fit together,
it was those two.

Miss Hallgrim whirled round. "Has a TROLL

wandered into our classroom or did that DISGUSTING noise come from one of YOU?"

"Sorry, Miss," said Hilda, raising her hand. "It won't happen again."

"You're right, Hilda, it won't," Miss Hallgrim said. "Because you will be standing outside in the HALLWAY until the BELL RINGS."

Hilda stood in the hallway, fuming. Why did the teacher not like her? she wondered. Was it because she asked Miss Hallgrim too many questions, or was it because she hardly ever accepted Miss Hallgrim's answers?

The bell rang suddenly, making Hilda jump. That was another thing about Trolberg. Wherever you went there was always some sort of bell ringing or bonging or trilling or donging.

The classroom door burst open and Trevor and his friends rushed out. Trevor was the class bully and he seemed to have taken a strong dislike to Hilda.

"Look who it is, guys!" Trevor said. "It's the stoat

decorator! Hey, Stoat Girl, tell us again why you moved to Trolberg?"

"Our cabin in the wilderness got stepped on by a giant," said Hilda in a small voice.

"Stepped on by a giant!" Trevor cackled. "I'll never get tired of hearing that. Catch you later, Stoat Girl!" With that, he gave Hilda a stinging flick on the ear and sprinted off down the hallway.

Frida and David were next out. Hilda had seen David around the place but she had hardly ever spoken to him, other than to tell him he had a bug on his head, which he usually did.

"You've got a bug on your head," said Hilda now.

"Thanks." David reached up to brush it off.

Frida looked at Hilda. "Why did you say *stoat* instead of *float*?"

Hilda shrugged. "Your f's are too curly. They look like s's."

"No, they don't! My f's have just the right amount of curliness. Not to mention crossbars. Now get your bag and come with us."

"What? Come where?"

"To the Gorrill Gardens bell tower," said Frida, passing her a pair of binoculars. "We need to get up high and scour the land for interesting plants to take cuttings from."

"Why do we need plant cuttings?"

"For the Wonderful Trolberg exhibition, of course. Miss Hallgrim put us all in groups of three and you're with me and David here. We've already talked about it, and we've decided we're going to do a "Plants of Trolberg" exhibit."

"Actually, it was Frida who decided that," said David. "I couldn't get a word in edgewise."

"Nonsense," said Frida. "You were nodding the whole time. Now, Hilda, hurry up and get your bag. We need to be at the top of that bell tower before the sun sets, or we won't see any plants at all."

COLLECT ALL THE BOOKS IN THE HILDA SERIES ...

FICTION BOOKS

Written by Stephen Davies and illustrated by Seaerra Miller

Hilda and the Hidden People
Hilda and the Great Parade
Hilda and the Nowhere Space

GRAPHIC NOVELS

Written and illustrated by Luke Pearson

Hilda and the Troll
Hilda and the Midnight Giant
Hilda and the Bird Parade
Hilda and the Black Hound
Hilda and the Stone Forest
Hilda and the Mountain King

Discover more of Hilda's world at
www.hildabooks.com